What Game Shall We Play?

PAT HUTCHINS

A Mulberry Paperback Book
New York

FOR LAURA

Watercolor paints and a black pen
were used for the full-color art.
The text type is ITC Symbol Medium.

The Library of Congress has cataloged
the Greenwillow Books edition of
What Game Shall We Play? as follows:
Hutchins, Pat. What game shall we play? /
by Pat Hutchins.   p. cm.
Summary: The animals ask each other what game
they should play, but only Owl has an answer.
ISBN 0-688-09196-2.
ISBN 0-688-09197-0 (lib. bdg.)
[1. Animals—Fiction.] I. Title.
PZ7.H96165Wg 1990 [E]—dc20
89-34621 CIP AC

3   5   7   9   10   8   6   4   2
First Mulberry Edition, 1994
ISBN 0-688-13573-0

Duck and Frog went out to play.
"What game shall we play?" asked Duck.
"I don't know," said Frog.
"Let's go and ask Fox."

So off they went to look for Fox.
Duck looked across the fields,
but he wasn't there.

Frog looked among the tall grass,

and there he was.

"What game shall we play, Fox?"
they asked.
"I don't know," said Fox.
"Let's go and ask Mouse."

So off they went to look for Mouse.
Duck looked over the wall,
but Mouse wasn't there.
Frog looked under the wall,
but she wasn't there, either.

So Fox looked in the wall,

and there she was.

"What game shall we play, Mouse?"
they asked.
"I don't know," said Mouse.
"Let's go and ask Rabbit."

So off they went to look for Rabbit.
Duck looked near his hole,
Frog looked on top of the hole,
Fox looked around the hole,

and Mouse looked in the hole,

and there he was.

"What game shall we play, Rabbit?"
 they asked.
"I don't know," said Rabbit.
"Let's go and ask Squirrel."

So off they went to look for Squirrel.
Duck looked behind the tree,
Frog looked in front of the tree,
Fox looked up to the top of the tree,
Mouse looked under the tree,

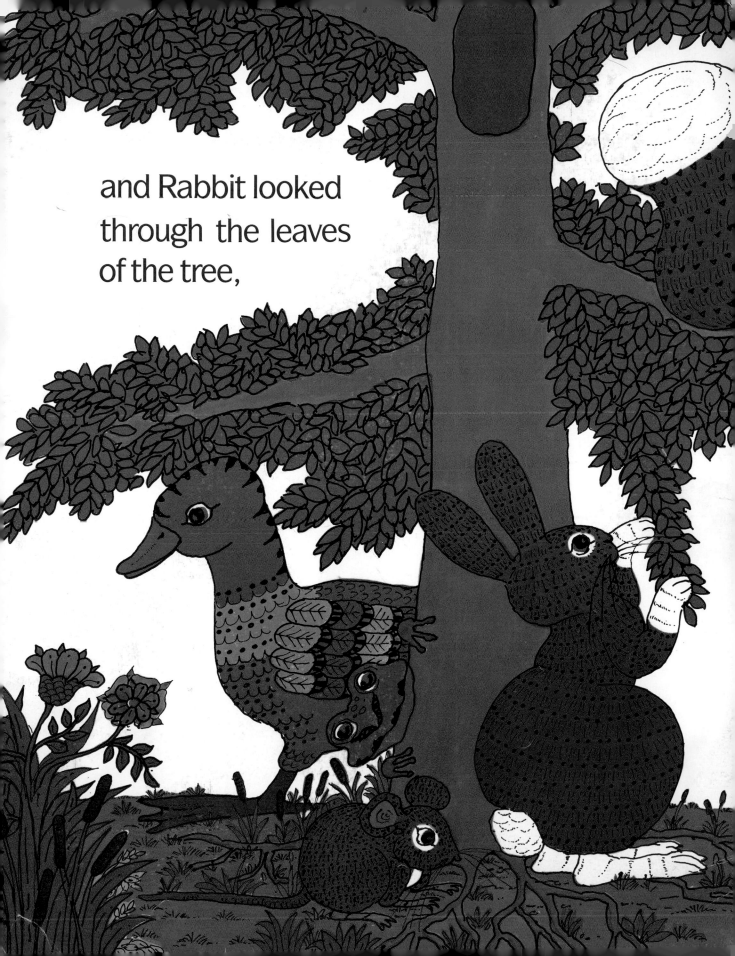

and Rabbit looked
through the leaves
of the tree,

and there she was.

"What game shall we play, Squirrel?"
 they asked.
"I don't know," said Squirrel.
"Let's find Owl and ask him."

But Owl found them first.
"What game shall we play, Owl?"
they asked.
"Hide and seek," said Owl.

And while Owl closed his eyes,
Duck and Frog hid in the pond,
Fox hid in the long grass,
Mouse hid in the wall,
Rabbit hid in the hole,
and Squirrel hid in the leaves in the tree.

Then Owl went to look for them.